A Portrait of the IAS As A Young Man

A Collection of Short Essays

A Portrait of the IAS As A Young Man

A Collection of Short Essays

NAVEEN KUMAR CHANDRA (IAS)

PRABHAT
PRAKASHAN

Published by
PRABHAT PRAKASHAN PVT. LTD.
4/19 Asaf Ali Road,
New Delhi-110 002 (INDIA)
e-mail: prabhatbooks@gmail.com

ISBN 978-93-5562-066-8
A PORTRAIT OF THE IAS AS A YOUNG MAN
by Naveen Kumar Chandra (IAS)

Edition
First, 2023

Price
₹ 250 (Rupees Two Hundred Fifty Only)

Printed at
Japan Art, Delhi

“ Like someone wise once said, the most crucial words are, “Indian” and “Service”.

To my father, whose dream
I am living.

Author's Note

Dear Readers,

It is with great pleasure and a sense of profound responsibility that I present to you "A Portrait of the IAS as a Young Man" This book delves into the captivating journey of a young civil servant as he steps into the dynamic world of the Indian Administrative Service (IAS), a path filled with unexpected challenges and rewarding experiences.

As a serving IAS officer, I have had the privilege of witnessing the inner workings of the civil service firsthand, and I felt compelled to share the trials and triumphs that young officers encounter while serving in the field. "A Portrait of the IAS as a Young Man" is a labor of love, drawing from my own experiences, to bring forth a compelling narrative that resonates with authenticity and human emotion.

The story revolves around the life of our protagonist, Naveen (myself), an idealistic and ambitious young IAS officer, whose journey mirrors the trials faced by many individuals stepping into public service. Through Naveen's eyes, we explore the corridors of power, where decisions shape lives and destinies, and where lofty ideals often collide with the stark realities of governance.

Throughout these pages, you will witness Naveen's struggles and expectations, the momentous learning curves, and the occasional brushes with reality that challenge his very core. You will accompany him as he navigates the intricate web of bureaucratic complexities, where every decision carries weighty consequences, and where the stakes are not merely personal but also impact the lives of countless citizens.

Moreover, "A Portrait of the IAS as a Young Man" is not just a journey through professional endeavors; it also delves deeply into Naveen's personal struggles. The book explores the delicate art of balancing personal aspirations with the demands of an all-consuming career, and the sacrifices one must make in pursuit of a greater purpose.

As you turn each page, I hope you find solace in the universality of Naveen's experiences - the moments of doubt, the revelations of purpose, and the discovery of profound meaning in the service of others. Through his story, I seek to encapsulate the essence of the human experience within the realm of public service, where compassion, resilience, and self-reflection emerge as guiding beacons.

It is my sincere wish that "A Portrait of the IAS as a Young Man" not only offers you a glimpse into the enigmatic world of civil service but also inspires you to reflect upon your own personal dance between the diverse facets of life. May the experiences shared within these pages serve as a catalyst for positive change, urging us all to contribute to a more compassionate and equitable world.

Thank you, dear readers, for embarking on this transformative journey with me. May "A Portrait of the IAS as a Young Man" spark a flame within each of us to embrace the beauty of the service and find meaning in our own unique paths.

With warmest regards,

– Naveen Kumar Chandra (IAS)

❖❖❖

Acknowledgements

As I stand on the threshold of completing this profound and introspective journey that is "A Portrait of the IAS as a Young Man," I am filled with a deep sense of gratitude and humility. This book is not just a collection of stories; it is a testament to the shared experiences and resilience of countless individuals who have been part of this transformative expedition.

First and foremost, I am profoundly grateful to my father, who dreamt of serving as a civil servant and who made it possible for me to do so. My other family members, my mother, sisters and my loving wife, all of you have been pillars of strength throughout this journey. Your unwavering support and belief in my endeavors have been a source of inspiration and hope.

To the citizens and communities in the field, who opened their hearts and lives to the young officers, I offer my heartfelt appreciation. Your stories, struggles, and aspirations have been the cornerstone of this narrative, reminding us of the profound responsibility that comes with serving the public.

I am immensely thankful to the myriad colleagues, civil servants, and administrative staff who work tirelessly behind the scenes to uphold the ideals of the IAS. Your dedication to public service and your unyielding commitment to the welfare of the nation serve as a beacon of hope for all.

To the editorial team and all those involved in the publishing process, I express my sincere gratitude. Your meticulous attention to detail and dedication to crafting a meaningful narrative have breathed life into this book, allowing it to reach the hands of readers worldwide.

To the readers of "A Portrait of the IAS as a Young Man," I extend my warmest appreciation. Your curiosity and willingness to immerse yourselves in the lives of a young officer validate the importance of sharing these experiences. May my stories inspire you to embrace the essence of public service, compassion, and the pursuit of a harmonious balance between personal and professional life.

With a heart brimming with gratitude and respect, I offer this book as a tribute to the collective journey of all those who walk the path of the IAS.

❖❖❖

Contents

❖❖❖

CHAPTER 1

Welcome to Bharat

"The real India is supposed to be living in its villages, well it's only half true, it's more surviving than living."

I was told that the driver would meet me at the station and his number was shared with me along with the details of the vehicle which led me to think, in case I am unable to contact the driver, am I supposed to search for the vehicle or to insist that I'll go only in the car with the said number plate if the driver brought any other car? When you have time, your mind wanders and I had just read a few chapters of a book and had pretty much nothing to do. So I was thinking all kinds of stuff, weird, crazy, outright nonsensical, all of it.

Anyway, as soon as the train entered Malda station, I thought of calling the driver to check if he had reached.

"Hello, are you Rakesh, the driver? Have you reached the station? The train will stop on platform no. 2 in about 5 minutes". I wasn't able to hear much of what he said due to the loud noise of what I was sure would have been the endless human sea present at any Indian railway station in any city of any state across the country. Also, while you are trying to de-board a train in India, you'd see, there appear out of nowhere, hundreds of people on the platform who make it even tougher to hear anything. But I was able to make out that he had reached the station. The train stopped and I got out of the train with my wife who was travelling with me and she was as excited as I was. In fact, she was much more excited, an excitement which was to battle a few bouts of disappointments fairly soon.

We got off and I called the driver again, he was looking for us as well and after about 10-12 minutes, he finally spotted us. A young lad, a few years younger than me as I later discovered. Thankfully he spoke comprehensible Hindi as I was still trying (not as hard I must confess) to pick up Bengali. He took a bag, I carried one and Anjana carried another one. From the look of the station, one could hardly tell Malda any different or apart from any other city in India, except the metros.

Too many people for too little infrastructure, small shops, rickshaws all over the place, more rickshaws than humans for some reason and more e-rickshaws than the manually operated ones (or as they are known here, a

"Toto") for another reason, narrow roads, vehicles parked almost all over the place, people in a hurry and of course, the perpetual cloud of a stampede about to happen. From the vehicle, my IAS probationer's brain had already got to work.

"Hmm, so waste management is an issue here, but where is it not an issue? I'll take up a project on the same. Oh yes, I'll try and see if we can do something on the lines of Indore. I am sure something must be going on, some plan of action must be in place. I'll be meeting the Collector on Monday, I'll ask him. Oh wait though, this is not a new issue, I am sure a lot must have been done, let me first see the existing things (the academy "gyan" would always knock on the door, they teach you to always read the existing policies first, common sense but more often one tends to forget the basics in excitement and common sense is just not as common as you'd wish it to be. Thus, reinvention of the wheel is done every year in every government office). You are so naive, like so many officers before me wouldn't have done anything right, like I am the chosen one, stop thinking yourself as the saviour already, try and learn as much as possible or at least don't act oversmart or smug. You idiot, don't try to run before you walk." The place was all right, I had already inquired about the existence of malls, multiplexes, etc, answer to all of that was a clear and loud no, but a "Vishal Mega Mart" did exist, the new hot spot for the people in Malda.

"I will take you to Bishal Mega Mart, sir. It's not far, I can take you in 5 minutes. I used to drive a bus in Kolkata, you will have no problems with me", the driver, Rakesh said with a smile. Not that pretty a sight though, given his teeth were an abstract art of red, yellow and black, a rather common sight with Indian men, it really did make both, "the zuban and the daant kesari". Anyway, the circuit house, the place which was to be my residence for the next one year, was not far and we reached the place in about 20 minutes. Before my service days started, I haven't really been to a government rest house or circuit house but since I got into the Indian Railways first and then the IAS, training had taken me all over the country. I have stayed in all sorts of government accommodation and trust me when I say this, you could spot one from a distance. It's like these place have a life of their own. A few vehicles always at the entrance, people checking in and out all the time, caretakers or cooks or helpers moving all over, all the time (though this was somehow only when someone new and important has checked in. I was not going to fall in either category as there is mostly a probationer there in districts and in the order of importance, the probationer is well I'd rather not say).

They all have paintings and showpieces from the "circuit house catalogue, spring to autumn for eternity collection" and your quintessential room furniture, a bed, a study table with a chair, a sofa, a table, a wardrobe, a small TV and an AC (it was a huge relief)." We were taken to our room, it was a small room, given that we were to stay there for a year, it was really going to be a problem I could sense that already. For the first few seconds only it seemed adequate and as far as "things" go, perhaps it was. I could sense Anjana was already half way through the list of things we'd be needing. I knew that I would have to make quite a few visits to the market in the coming days.

We were then given a set of information by the caretaker, "sir, you can ring the bell and someone will come for sure, you'll have to inform in advance if you'd need food prepared, there is no washing machine so you'll have to wash your own clothes. If you need anything, there are many shops just outside the main gate, a huge market is also nearby. The collectorate is only 5 minutes from here sir." I was impressed, this man had seen many IAS probationers and he knew almost all the doubts that I could have. He knew the doubts, not solutions and it was to give me a real headache later for certain things.

I messaged the collector as soon as we arrived and he acknowledged, but to my surprise he had asked me to accompany him to a field visit the very next day. I was, to be really honest, ecstatic, I mean who would've thought right, that my first day in the city, my day "-2" as Assistant Collector and I was already called to accompany the

Collector to visit a flood hit area. I was not at all surprised but I was indeed happy to know that my stay was not going to be a passive one.

I was happy that the Collector had asked me to join and accompany him to a flood hit area on what was not yet my first day of my stint there. All probationers want their district training to be exciting and I was certainly getting a great start. I was supposed to reach the Collectorate at 8 am the next day, Sunday, it was July 28, 2019.

❖❖❖

CHAPTER 2

Into The Field

"Till you've gone inside and paid your dues, its like that spectator who watches a sport on TV and shouts his perfect advice after watching a slow motion replay"

When you land in the district on a Saturday, you are surely not expecting to go to a flood hit area on a Sunday, surely you react with a lot of happiness and excitement at the start you get but it is definitely a surprise.

But then you are also expected to expect the unexpected, in the IAS, that's how your life is going to be henceforth, so a solid start on that front.

I had reached Malda late on the previous Saturday and as soon as I reached my room, I had messaged the District Collector. He had asked me to accompany him on a field visit the next morning. Malda has had this age-old problem of annual flooding, and this year was to be no different. The collector was going to a flood-affected area, to inspect how the relief work was going, to assess the damage and to listen to the problems that people faced.

Although he had given me a choice, the tone of the conversation was very friendly, but if your Collector had asked you to do something, it really was not a choice for you to make, not that I wanted to make one, I was very excited.

I woke up early, did my morning routine and reached the office quite early. We were to assemble at the Collectorate and leave from there. From the Collectorate I was asked to reach the BDO office of the concerned Block of the flood hit area.

A block is the most important unit of district administration in the state of Bengal. Well, I asked my driver but he had no clue, it turned out, he was new to the city as well. I tried to look it up in the map and to some relief, it was present in the map. But to add to the confusion, we didn't know which of the two "Ratuas" we were supposed to go, there were two of them, "Ratua 1" block and "Ratua 2" block.

Anyway, I called up my orderly, which turned out to be some exercise, this guy happened to speak only and strictly very authentic and to me very exotic Bengali, which was a struggle for me to understand, even more so on a telephonic conversation.

Well, somehow I got to know that he didn't know which block I was supposed to go either. So, I finally called up one of the other district officers, and he told me where exactly we were to go. I told the same to the driver and he was able to find the route. Though straightforward, Indians have a fascinating way of complicating even the simplest of routes, someway or the other, we would love to come up with a shorter and easier way to reach there, even though most often than not, we'd end up confusing even ourselves and would consult four more people before saying, "reach this place and ask someone about that place, from that placc, it's only this much."

Well, we reached there, it took us two hours, yes, that far, within the district itself and it was still not the farthest block. The Collector had of course managed to reach before, I was sure I had left earlier, but then, of course, the Collector was not stopping at every 500 metres asking for directions.

I was quite angry with the driver and the person who decided to give me a driver who didn't know the basic places I'd need to go, I was expected to be on the field and I can't be asking directions all the time. But I calmed myself down. As I reached there, staff and officers from district administration somehow knew me already and requested me to go inside the BDO's chamber. I saw many officers sitting, not standing, in attention. As I entered, everyone looked at me and the Collector looked at me and asked me to sit, I acknowledged everyone and took a seat. It turned out, there were local elected representatives as well in the room.

After a briefing which lasted about 15 minutes, we left. It wasn't tough this time, we were to follow the collector's vehicle. We drove for 15 minutes, it was the most rural area I've seen in years, that is since I last visited my paternal grandparents' place.

Narrow streets, more cows and goats than humans, clean yet dirty, people going about their business, moving at snail's pace. As we got closer, more and more people began to appear. A huge crowd was awaiting the collector, they were furious over some matter and I got to know what exactly made them feel that way. As soon as we reached, I could hear a loud noise, the one that the crowd makes, coming from a gathering but the noise vanished and was replaced by a loud hush as soon as the collector alighted. All this while, my only task was, to observe the way the collector handled the issue. There were too many people, there were police personnel at the venue but no where adequate to handle anything, if anything was to go wrong.

As I stood there, looking as far as I could, I could see only water, breaching everything, every wall, every checkdam, every other obstruction put in its way, on purpose or by accident, the water was furious and it seemed as if it was getting worse.

We all sat down, in a shed there itself, and the collector started noting things down and issuing some instructions, about relief and steps to be taken to contain the damage. One very interesting thing which I saw was, though the people were angry but they were very respectful, they listened patiently and waited for their turn to speak. What was also amazing was the fact that they had trust and faith in the administration, one might expect they would have lost it by now but they were reasonable enough to understand that it was a natural occurrence and only so much was in the hands of the administration. It was indeed a task for the collector though, to manage the people, the administration, the elected representatives and at the same time, keep himself composed. As we left the place, he asked me to join him in his car.

It was an eventful day and as we drove back, he asked me about myself and told me, "you'll have, in your career, in the next few years, many things to do but always focus on the things which deal with the livelihood of the people, that must be your priority". I couldn't agree more. He also showed me a board and asked me, "See this, do you know what it is? Always try to spot these boards on your visits, they will tell you what exactly these schemes are, under what projects or scheme they were undertaken (it was a MGNREGS CCR road). I nodded and we proceeded back.

It was evening already and as I look back, it was not short of a Baptism by Fire, technically by water, so a regular Baptism maybe.

❖❖❖

CHAPTER 3

On Time

"Time is not one of the things, it is the only thing".

Something was very strange about the morning that day. I had just woken up but somchow it felt I was already up and getting ready for sometime now, like a zombie, I had woken up hours ago, it was not a lazy morning but surely a slow one. There was a clear sense of urgency in the air, but a slow urgency, it was supposed to be perfect but not a rash kind of an urgency. I remember I didn't sleep properly either, restless the whole time, just wanting to be on time and everything to be perfect. Still, I didn't feel exhausted or anything of that sort. Somehow the excitement and nervousness had trumped everything else. It was going to be my first day at my first job, a job that had not come easily.

So my first hint should have been the surprise in the voice of my driver when I called him and asked him to reach my home by 8:30 am in the morning. I remember him saying, "Sir, aapnake officaer aage kothaou jete hobe?" Or something on the same lines, meaning "sir, do you have to go anywhere before going to the office?". Maybe it had something to do with the fact that I wasn't yet fluent enough with Bengali, and Bengali spoken in a typical rural accent was even tougher that I didn't get that he was not trying to ask but in fact questioned the whole premise of the call, so early, for office, what for.

I had woken my wife up as well, she likes sleeping so I remember distinctly, her telling me, "you have office, why is it that I have to get up?'. She was absolutely correct but my restlessness had made me wake her up as well why should I be miserable alone, lets be miserable together. I was nervous yes and she could sense, reassuring me after every few minutes that, "It'd be great" and "don't worry, just relax".

So, I was ready and in my car at 8:50 sharp. I still clearly remember the time as I had forgotten my watch which gave me a mini heart attack as I thought I would definitely get late. Plus how poorly it would speak of an IAS officer who doesn't wear a watch, it would mean I didn't care for time and here I was, sitting in the car at 8:50 am in the morning. I saw the time on my phone and rushed back up to get my watch. Though the office was just 5 minutes away, I still wanted to be there at 9 am sharp. As the car approached the main entrance of the Collectorate (the office of the District Collector and District Magistrate), I got my second hint. There was literally no one there, not a soul. I was shocked yes, not surprised and for a moment I was like, "Rakesh, is it a holiday today that I am not aware of?", to which he said, "Sir, I don't know", I was like what does he know and was frustrated by now, quite visibly.

I have been to a Collectorate before, and you can almost sense one from a mile before you actually get there. It is as if the entire city is headed there for some reason. Only, there was no one there today, not just people but no guards, no security, no one. So, I asked my driver again, "where is everyone?" and he replied, this time sensing what I was talking about, "sir, it's too early, no one will come for another 45-50 minutes".

Then suddenly I remembered, the timings of the offices being discussed in the academy, it was obviously a subject of discussion there. Once you got your cadres (cadre is where you are supposed to serve for most of your service life), you'd hear a great deal about every cadre and rumours would get a fresh breath of life. They were almost like part of the snow on the mountains in Mussoorie, they'd come down every year, and every year, the innocent and fresh OTs (Officer Trainees) would be taken by surprise, in shock and in awe in equal measure. Bengal had its own set of rumours, as a matter of fact, if there is a single state which was talked about the most, it was Bengal.

So, I get out, open the gate and call my orderly. I am sure I caught him in his sleep, he lived nearby though so he could afford to sleep that late. He assured me he would be there in 30 minutes. I was only lucky that my chamber, for some reason, wasn't locked. So I got there and waited. I waited for the entire office to arrive, it was 9 am in the morning. One by one people start coming and I could sense them talking about this "weird, new officer" who had come at 9. But they'd soon come to know I was a probationer and pardon me for my ignorance.

❖❖❖

CHAPTER 4

The Pandemic: Covid Diaries

"Times come, once in centuries, when the focus of the entire humankind is shifted on ensuring survival, on ensuring that lives are not lost, on ensuring that we save as many as possible, it was one such time".

A global pandemic doesn't happen overnight, but then, even though we were witnessing the events unfold all over the world, when it finally spread in India, when people in our neighbourhood started getting sick, that is when we knew it was there. I still remember, when the nationwide lockdown was announced, most of us at some level were expecting it but when it was announced, it still came as a surprise as you expect that the worst will not happen to you, and a lockdown was not bad in itself but it signalled that things were truly very serious and any measure would now not be out of bounds. It appeared as if everything was about to change.

I clearly remember that I was in my independent charge as a BDO, a charge you are supposed to handle during training to get hands on experience at the cutting edge of administration. It was now suddenly, my responsibility to ensure that lockdown norms were adhered to, that in my block, people with symptoms were taken care of, quarantine centres and hospitals run smoothly, that there is enough for everyone to eat and yes, that most works of a typical government office continue without hiccups.

But this was also a time when I felt helpless for the first time. I was by now used to getting hundreds of calls on my official number as a BDO normally gets them, but soon they were too many. The phone rang 24 hours and they had now started calling even my personal number. But, I would answer each and every call and hear the person out, a principle which I follow till date. Most of them were locals from the block, but many were from other parts of the district and some even from other districts of the state. They were stuck somewhere in the and were hoping to come back. I could help many but on several occasions, it was not in my hands. Though in all cases I tried connecting them with the relevant authorities but at times they couldn't be helped as fast as I desired or they wanted. That's when

I felt helpless. I could hear them cry and at times I cried with them.

I remember clearly that people would send me pictures of the places they were stuck at, that they had no food and no money left. I would try and connect them with local administration with the help of my batchmates or seniors in the service there. Most of them did get relief but many didn't. The reasons were many but mostly it happened in the case of individuals who were difficult to locate or were on the move and this was a massive emergency of a scale which no one had actually seen before and people were in a constant panic mode.

It was not easy. Perhaps the biggest challenge civil administration has faced for a long time, or perhaps ever, it was as if we were in a war and this time the enemy was well within the border. I would leave home daily, visit hospitals, quarantine centres, knowing very well that I could get infected and that I might just pass it on to my wife. It was tough. But then, "this is why you joined the service", you'd tell yourself and go on with it.

The Covid battle, which still continues, was fought and led by doctors, healthcare workers and ground level staff of various departments who worked selflessly. I know it first hand, my younger sister is a doctor and I know how much of a risk she took. She worked with the government in a district hospital during the lockdown. But I am glad that I played an extremely minute and small part in it. I am glad that the service gave me this opportunity.

I remember that during preparation days, I would at times just sit and wonder how life would be after getting into the IAS. I suppose all aspirants do that. I would think, " I'd do this and do that, oh wait, it would be a new challenge every day. I'd handle Development, Empowerment, Schemes, Law and Order, I'd get to see so much", but I never imagined this. This pandemic did something for us, specifically for our batch, it showed us and taught us a lot, much of which is otherwise taught over years. We were suddenly not boys and girls anymore, we were men and women.

I can very firmly say that, to join the service only because it gives prestige or power or respect or fame is a very superficial logic. Instead to join it because it gives you the satisfaction of helping so many individuals must be the driving force. To join the service as one will get a driver or a cook or a guard but to join it because one will get a responsibility to make an actual contribution must be the reason. Because, once one joins for the satisfaction and the responsibility, all the other things don't matter and surely one does get the perks but one wouldn't care for them.

❖❖❖

CHAPTER 5

May the Force be with You

"To think you can change the world is good, to think you don't need the world is foolish."

Illcgal Sand Mining is onc of thosc issucs which have seen a tremendous amount of media attention and at times a few lethal accidents as well. It is said that wherever it is carried out, it nurtures and runs a parallel economy where they have the support of the local people.

I never imagined my first week as SDM and SDO would be so exciting and challenging as it turned out to be.

My sub division sees the maximum amount of sand mining among all sub divisions in the district and in fact one of the highest in the state. The sand mining though is not illegal, what is though illegal is the mining over and above the allowed limit and the overloading, paying a small fine and getting away with thousands of rupees worth of minerals and at the same time causing environmental damage and harm to our roads due to the overloading.

So to check all this, the district administration decided to start a very aggressive campaign. To check illegal sand mining, overloading and the plying of vehicles long past their legal age, ones which should not be on the road. There are obviously many other major and minor issues which arise when such a campaign is planned. These people are very smart, almost always finding a way out. They know very well that the administration has several other things and many of them are much more important and that they can't be looking here all the time.

You also have reluctant officers, an apprehensive staff and inertia, to solve an issue which could do without all of this. Anyway, we have to start somewhere.

On one such occasion, the land officials in my sub division were asked to go and serve notices to people who had stacked illegal sand on the road side, one of the illegal acts they were involved in and one which was also a cause of many accidents. They were instructed to take adequate force but somehow this time they didn't.

What happened next was fairly predictable, I got a letter telling me how the land official was surrounded by hundreds of people, and was threatened. He had to run for his life.

While it was his fault that he didn't take any force with him and didn't follow the SOP, it was nonetheless not justified and absolutely criminal for anyone to attack or threaten or intervene when a government official is trying to do his job, it's a punishable offence.

I had made my mind and I would not let this pass. I had the backing of the district administration, so I made an elaborate plan.

I called the land officials, the transport officials, police officials to my office the next day early in the morning. I didn't tell them why or that I had asked others to come as well, of course they knew but they didn't know where we were going. When I reached my office I had all of them come there one by one, slightly surprised but aware that it was going to be a sudden raid, they still didn't know where though.

I called the land official who was threatened as well and asked him to take us to the same spot. We arrived there in 20 minutes, this time though we were not alone, and I was there as well.

This time they were taken by surprise, strange that they had seen a solo raid only a few days ago, such was the audacity. We were able to catch them red-handed and in fact, illegally transporting the illegally stacked sand. As soon as the driver of the earth moving vehicle, a JCB vehicle, saw us from a distance, he tried to get off and run away. But we got hold of all the men there and the driver was soon called to the scene by those apprehended by us. The Motor Vehicles Inspector in the meanwhile checked for all the documents and found that the JCB was in violation of almost all the requirements there were under the Motor Vehicles Act and to add to that it also indulged in gross violation of the Mines and Minerals Act, so it was seized.

We decided to move ahead on the same road and serve notices to all those who stacked sand illegally. On my next stop, yet again, multiple dumpers and a JCB were impounded but the real fun began when the owners turned up. One could see how human psychology works, they tried all the tricks they had. Of course when nothing worked they almost begged us to let their vehicles go.

I was of course not there to let them go, not that I had that power anyway. It was not for me to decide but the relevant authorities, in this case the courts. I had tried my best to maintain the element of surprise but by the time we got to our third or fourth spot, the media had reached there. I decided to leave for another meeting, instructing another officer there to keep moving ahead and keep the process well documented and recorded, to keep me posted of all happenings and to continue serving notices till the end of the day.

It was a fantastic exercise and we ended up serving some of the biggest offenders and seized multiple JCBs and Dumpers. Though the issue is so complicated and so many people involved that one raid hardly ever does anything to put a stop to these activities. But it was surely going to instil some fear and it was also going to send a message and a signal that things might not be the same anymore.

❖❖❖

CHAPTER 6

Incremental vs. Revolutionary

"To change things for millions of people deprived for hundreds of years, incremental is not the answer".

If you were to ask me what is the one thing which makes the service worth joining, while there are many things, big and small. However if I were to pick one, I'd say that the it offers the power and responsibility to hear the common man and with it the power to help him.

It's very easy to say "I'll see" and then forget or ignore or delay or even just refuse later. But then when anyone reaches out to us, anyone, we must know that they have perhaps come to us after exhausting the other options. They have come to us hoping that maybe we will listen, they have come to us thinking this is where they'll get some sense of justice.

This, this one thing makes everything worth it for me.

Every time we help a poor man, every time we correct a wrong long overdue, every time we lift someone up, we install in them the faith in the system. That is the only thing I tell aspirants now, nothing else, that once they enter the service, never ever forget this. I tell them, once they enter the service, to enjoy it but also to remember why they came to the service and from where they came. I tell them, all the fame, the glamour and the followers on social media are of no use and if they can't use their service and their position or power or whatever one wishes to call it, to do what they said they'd do once selected, to the interview board. I ask them to always remember that when they help even a single individual, they help the world become a better place, when they respond, they give hope. And like the famous dialogue goes, hope is reassuring.

❖❖❖

CHAPTER 7

What Makes A Good Officer?

"The simplest of things matter the most, in the end it is all about kindness, compassion and empathy".

It is a question, the answer to which would seem straightforward but it isn't. One might say honesty, well of course, but honesty to whom? Is it just that you need to be honest to the service, to the people, the staff or is it a broader concept, whereby you are to remain honest to yourself more than anyone else. Some might say devotion to duty is an important thing, true, it is a very important thing. But devotion to duty would first need us to define what duty exactly is, it is very complicated, not as simple as one might expect. Then there is integrity, another pillar of the social value system and surely one on which the foundations of the civil services is built, one which we have come to recognise as indispensable, well it absolutely is. However more often that not, what looks like a strong pillar is nothing but a rust-ridden structure, what seems like a huge tree is nothing but a shallow trunk, integrity perhaps has seen better days. So what is it, well all of the above mentioned traits or values are important, not trying to discount them at all. But it is no secret and secret keeping is not that tough, in fact in bureaucracy there are no secrets, that anyone even talking about all the values discussed above is dismissed as idealistic and immature. Apart from all the values already discussed, what I have come to realise as the most important quality of an officer is if he or she has empathy for the poor. Not to say that the well off don't need or deserve empathy, they do of course but that the poor have nothing else, no expectations at all.

In my experience, I find it very saddening that people are almost shocked (in a good and odd way) that someone in my position is actually answering all their calls or replying to their random WhatsApp queries or meeting every single person who comes to meet as often as they want to and for as long as they wish, hearing them out patiently. Trust me, time is not an issue.

The issue is that people are afraid of being kind. They are afraid of being perceived as weak if they show emotion and empathise. They are afraid of doing things which are perceived to be not "their job", which in fact exactly is their job but then anyway.

What then is the point? The point is this, please be kind to people. More so if one is in a position of privilege or desire to be in one. Listen to them. Try to solve their problems.

You can be everything but if you can't be kind to a stranger who has nothing to offer you in return, what use is anything else that you do? Nothing at all.

❖❖❖

CHAPTER 8

Don't Become What You Hated

"Well now that I have made it, the same standards don't apply to me anymore"

Not very long ago, I was prcparing for UPSC CSE. While preparation, I used to always wonder, how come so many government officers have no empathy at all, what happens to them once they enter the services? What is the reason that they can refuse pleas, can deny requests and can ignore tears? I always wondered would I become the same once I entered the service.

The problem with this line of thought can be appreciated in a much better way once someone enters the service and gets to experience how it is on the other side or perhaps gets to read an honest assessment from within, I shall try to write one here, as honest as possible. I am not going to deny the lack of empathy in an appreciable number of officers, just like any group of people. Most officers though have an issue, they forget that it is the position or the chair or the service that people are respectful of or afraid of and not them as an individual. No one cares about them per se but their chair. They forget this.

Whenever someone approaches an officer for any work or help or assistance or anything, in their mind of course, they are absolutely right and justified in asking for what they are asking for. It is not their fault either, it's basic human nature. Just ask yourself if you have ever cursed someone for doing their duty and blamed them for misusing their powers (when at most what they did was use it well within their right only that you were at the receiving end and did not get what you wanted).

For example, someone is stopped by a traffic policeman for not wearing a helmet and is given a fine, he would then curse the officer for using his power and not trying to understand or listen to his "issue" or not agreeing to just let one go just this one time or something of that sort. Of course there is another side to it but this and incidents like this happen almost universally, with everyone.

The issue is, if you come to an officer asking for a favour, and he refuses, and you think well how rude of him or that he lacks empathy, you should just ask yourself two questions, first, would you be fine if he favoured someone else and treated you like the rest and second, how would anything function if everyone comes seeking a favour or to cut the line? Of course, there can be and there are emergencies, there are exceptions and these cases must be treated as such and viewed with empathy by the officers, which does not happen often and hence the issue. But why does it not happen, there is a problem there as well.

The problem is, once someone is treated preferentially, it would surely not end there. Other people would either think that it happened due to some strings being pulled somewhere or perhaps some other quid pro quo was in place. The issue is that even an exception made due to an actual emergency, on purely humanitarian grounds would not go down so well with people other than those who had the emergency and needed help and were in a position to understand. This is because that most people, other than officers too, lack empathy for their fellow citizens. It's very easy to notice, just see how many are comfortable with someone cutting a line in a bank citing an emergency, not many. In fact people start saying things like, "What emergency? Even I have an emergency, let me go to" or "How do I know you have an emergency" or "I don't care, there is an emergency at all our homes", it is very common.

I am not trying to discount for the lack of kindness among the officers but this is a genuine issue. For example, hypothetically, if I am to favour one farmer over another, this one farmer wishes to sell his paddy ahead of others due to an emergency, even though he has a token and he will be able to sell it when his number comes, just like everyone else, but if I do allow him to sell early, the very next day I would have a huge list of applicants citing emergencies, all of which would have at least some measure of truth to them and also some paperwork to support their claim.

Now, if I were to deny the farmers after the first one with the emergency, the rest would point out that I did allow one, why did I do that? Did I favour him in return for something or was he someone special or someone powerful or what was the matter? When in fact all that happened was that the person had an emergency where he had a sick wife who needed an operation urgently, each day was important or else she could even die.

Now, if I was to allow all emergencies then any system in place would just collapse, I know how it sounds but it happens, it happened even during Covid travel restrictions when people would go out for nothing, at the peak, wandering around, risking everyone and on being apprehended saying they were out to get medicine when they had no prescriptions.

It is very easy, again, to say for example why not design a system which takes care of all such cases on a preferential basis and take them first? The problem with this line of reasoning is, for example in the illustration above is that the poor farmers for whom this and similar schemes are actually announced, all have some or the other issue at their homes. Also, how would one decide what constitutes a real emergency and what does not?, Perhaps there can be a list but then a case outside of it will surely come, what then? Its a never ending issue, one which will always have subjectivity and would be open to human discretion.

So, in practice, on the ground, systems don't seem to work as efficiently as one might think. The reasons for this are not what is generally thought. You can never design a fool proof process and you would eventually have to rely on humans. The point is, in the end, it will boil down to some person, some human would be required to take a decision in cases of exceptions or emergencies.

The reason why I decided to write this is because most comments about civil services and the way officers are, don't look or appreciate this aspect. While it is not a justification and much what is said is true but I feel it is something to think about. Most officers think on the lines that they can take up each and every case and look into it. But with all the other things they have to do, it becomes increasingly tough. Still, personally, as a personal work ethic which I have decided to embrace, I prefer to do this, to look into each and every individual case I get. Some prefer to focus more on other things. I deeply care about such exceptions but that doesn't mean that those who aren't able to look at each individual case don't care about them.

Both these ways of functioning are manageable of course, dealing with individual grievances and big schemes. However like all processes, the one which you will put in place to look after such cases, this too, would be open to being manipulated, being exploited and falling short at times. Nonetheless, I feel very strongly that a process to deal with such cases must be in place in all offices, it generally is there too, an elaborate grievance redressal system is there everywhere but it is needed to be run with considerable empathy.

When a civil servant gets a request where he can in fact help but then he is afraid of getting more such requests he is absolutely 100 per cent wrong in ignoring the request on this ground. But, the people should also appreciate that when an officer does get this request, where it is not an emergency, one of the reasons why he refuses to treat you preferentially is perhaps the principle of fairness.

This is one of the actual dilemmas of a civil servant, more so someone posted in the field.

❖❖❖

CHAPTER 9

No Leave for You!

"No amount of so-called perks make up for the time missed with your loved ones".

When you are an outsider in a completely new state, trying your best to adjust and get comfortable in a new culture, learn a new language and you live away from you family, mostly alone, getting to see them once or if you are fortunate, twice a year, you do become sensitive about leave. But that is the nature of our service, surely it doesn't even come close to say the armed forces but it would be unreasonable to deny that there is no sacrifice involved, no amount of facilities or so-called perks can make up for missed time with one's family.

Almost all government establishments at all levels have a very high shortage of staff, at times it is a wonder how these offices even manage to run and function, but then it is not a very simple problem. It can't just be solved by simply recruiting more people. This is one of the reasons, the shortage of the staff, that leave is very hard to come by, more so if you occupy a critical post, like if you are posted in the field. At the time of writing this, I had taken my last three days leave more than a year ago and haven't left the station for one entire day in almost 9 months. But that's a part of our service which we learn to accept and adjust to.

But, when I joined as SDO, I wanted to conduct a small experiment. I wanted to see how I can make my staff and officers more efficient and happy if I implement minor changes. One of them was, to implement a "no-questions asked" leave policy in my office. This would mean all staff and officers would just have to ask me once and they'd be allowed to avail themselves of the leave available to them, simple.

Now, for context, this is something almost unheard of in any office, let alone a government office, more so a SDM/ SDO office where we have year round responsibilities like Elections and electoral rolls, issuing of various certificates, monitoring development in our jurisdiction and of course the SDM court. It was thus very shocking to almost everyone when in the first meeting with the staff and officers I announced two things, first, my door is always open for every single person working at any level in the office to directly approach me in case they need any help and two, if one wishes to go on leave, just ask in time.

Now, some might expect that this would cause a complete mess and I'd be neck high in leave water but it didn't happen. In fact, over a period of 1.5 years, I saw a gradual and steady improvement in efficiency, general level of happiness and satisfaction and last but not the least a fierce loyalty to the office and to the job.

It was also amazing to see that people started to be more considerate themselves when to ask for leave and they asked when they actually needed it, almost taking on the responsibility to not "misuse" the leniency being shown. It was almost a race for staff to be increasingly present, it worked in the opposite direction. It does make sense now of course as the human mind works in a very complicated fashion. You give it something freely and the value of the gesture goes down. You deny it a certain thing and the value automatically shoots up. In most cases the classical economics of demand-supply works, higher the supply, and suddenly people don't fancy it as much.

Similarly, the morale of the staff which is otherwise under tremendous pressure to perform year round with little or no acknowledgement for the same also shoots up. In fact the image of a typical government servant is not that exemplary, when in fact most a really normal hard working citizens trying to work honestly for their living and in turn sacrificing a lot, family time, functions, important days and what not. The morale got a boost as a result of the open door policy and them knowing that they will be heard and shown empathy in case they needed some help. It made them happier to come to work, knowing that if needed they'd be given help and if needed, some one is there to hear them out.

This made the office staff fiercely loyal to the chair, not to me in particular but to the office of the SDO. They would do anything to ensure the work is done. I could see this as in almost every single government programme, the performance of the Sub Division went up, and it did so in all the blocks in the jurisdiction as well. Th policy was to help, support and empathise. No one wants to not perform, at least in most cases, so when something wrong heppens, there is an explanation and there is mostly a solution as well.

The no question asked leave policy has resulted in some very acceptable changes. The total number of leaves taken have gone down, no one even imagines to go on leave without informing or asking, no one takes any unnecessary leave, Efficiency of all staff has risen and the overall atmosphere and mood of the office is also much better.

What this minuscule experiment of mine told me was not just limited to the workplace and the efficiency of the office staff and employees but much beyond that. If we are to take care of the basic well-being of those who are in any way dependent on us, if we take responsibility and use our power to not subject anyone to it but to empower people we would not just get work done but make people happier and healthier.

Mental well-being of staff and employees is anyway, in my opinion, the responsibility of the head of the office. It is upto the head of the office to take measures to ease the load. While this experiment is not something which can be universally applied in all circumstances but certainly one of the other version of similar steps can surely be undertaken.

Some of them also need to be timely sanction of leaves, pensions, dues, etc. All these things cause tremendous anxiety to employees who have given most of their lives to their job.

We owe it to them.

❖❖❖

CHAPTER 10

A Case As Old As You

" Hope is perhaps the last thing to die but when it does, nothing else remains".

It is almost in vogue or a fashion to curse administration and anyone who has anything to do with it, be it civil officers, politicians, police or just about anyone. The reasons for the same are also not imaginary, most of the reasons are reasonable. At one point or another, all of us have cursed the "system" and its ways.

But once I entered the service, and got a chance to experience what it is like in the system, I got to see that frequently it is not the fault of the people handling the situation. This is not to say they have no responsibility for so many things that are wrong and must be changed but what I mean is that at times there is not much they can do.

But then you get to see something which makes you wonder and question everything that you have just discovered about the system.

One such thing that I saw was a case which was brought to my notice by an old couple. It was a "patta" case, which is the type of a legal document given by the government to the landless entitling them with ownership rights over a small parcel of land.

In this particular case, it was brought to my notice that this old man had been given a patta in the year 1992 but for some reason he was never given possession over the piece of land. He told me that he had been trying ever since but to no avail and has got nowhere with the same.

It was of course very absurd to listen to the claim. I mean anyone would say it makes no sense, why would he not be given possession on a piece of land which was according to him, free of any encroachment and did not have any pending civil suit at any level, it made no sense at all. What also didn't make any sense to me was that if one was to assume that there were some inexplicable circumstances and somehow he wasn't given possession due to those, why wasn't he given a patta somewhere else instead after trying a few times to settle him in the original place and failing to do so. Law has provisions of the same and surely there was no reason to keep him landless for 30 years. It all made no sense to me.

Thus, an inquiry was ordered to find out whatever they could about the case and submit a report to me.

What they found out was something out of a movie perhaps. Absurd and real at the same time. The case was a typical example of how things which we least imagine and perhaps only imagine even if we do, play a decisive role in the matters on ground.

After the report was submitted and I got to see the findings, I was amazed, shocked, surprised, all at once. Everything the couple had claimed was true, they were given the patta, they weren't given possession, there was no case or suit pending, they were never asked to take a patta anywhere else. The reason why they were never given a patta was the fact that the locality where the land was was dominated by a particular community and they belonged to another community. The locals didn't want anyone whom they considered not equal to them living with them and thus never allowed them to take over possession. Now, this is interesting as there was no legal way for them to prevent the couple to take possession as their reason itself was almost criminal, discriminatory. So, what they instead did was use their influence to just delay it indefinitely.

Authorities didn't do anything as they didn't want any "trouble". They didn't offer him another land as the old man was not prepared to go anywhere else as he said and rightly so, it was not just about land anymore but his dignity. I was also told that I was not the first officer the old couple had approached regarding the same issue. One can of course see that, 30 years is a long time and officers change every 1-2 years.

So, I had the report, I had the facts, and now I knew the actual reasons as well. What would one do in such circumstances? The safest is to say, “Ah, well, I’ll be transferred in a few months, why do I have to get into an issue which is so old and spoil things for myself, not my problem”, something perhaps which has made the case linger for so long in the first place. Another approach would have been to try and convince the old couple to take a patta somewhere else and just end the case with perhaps a “win” for everyone. But the old man was ready to die waiting for his right than to settle in some other place and it was of course not my job to find convenience over law.

And then, finally, to try and talk to the locals who have opposed his patta for all these years, many of the original opposition was in fact not alive anymore, but their families still opposed it. This would of course not mean to just leave it to their wisdom and decision but a step in ensuring that possession is indeed given to the patta holders. It would take considerable time and effort, would require multiple meetings and visits by different officers to the spot and help and cooperation from local leaders, police and civil society. But then it was the right thing to do, so that is what we did.

In a case as old as I was, an elderly couple who has almost given up all hope, was given what was theirs. They were given possession of the land and it was all done very peacefully, it took time yes, but it was done.

It was in fact that the spirit of the old couple who gave me the strength and inspiration to get them what was theirs to begin with.

❖❖❖

CHAPTER 11

I Need It Today

" When someone manages to reach out, beating all odds, with a legitimate request, they can't and shouldn't ever be sent back empty-handed".

India is a country of competitions and competitive exams. It would be difficult to find someone who is educated and has never appeared in any competitive exam in his life. You have to appear in one for entrance into a college or university of your choice, you have to appear in one for scholarships, you have to appear in one for higher education, another for your dream job and of course civil services.

These exams are all very different, for different things at different levels but they have certain features and elements in common. One of these things is the need for the applicants to provide for various kinds of documents in their applications, mostly certificates if they seek any kind of relaxation or benefit. Mostly caste certificates and EWS certificates for reservations, income and asset certificates, Non-Creamy Layer certificate, Residential and Domicile certificates, disability certificates, etc.

These certificates are very important for anyone belonging to any of those categories which is almost 85 percent to 90 percent of our population making them very important documents in general. Most people have thus over the years got into the habit of getting these made years in advance for their children as they know it might take time if they decide to get one at the last minute. Most states have also made these things online but still a component of inquiry and report remains which make it still a lengthy process, one which can't be made any shorter after a while. Still there are delays, which continue.

I remember getting a case where the applicant needed a certificate the same day. He applied for the same in the morning and needed it the same day as the last day to apply for the counselling was only the next day and he would miss out on that if he didn't get the certificate. In this scenario he applied and was told by the staff dealing with the certificate in my office that it would take a few days. He, on the other hand, wasn't prepared to listen to anyone.

Now, the boy approached me, with visible anger on his face that he needed the certificate the same day and he was being refused. What he said wasn't a lie, he indeed needed it the same day and he was indeed refused. In such a scenario though I couldn't say much to my staff, they didn't break any rule and they didn't know how to prioritise the applications, for all they knew someone else needed their's even more urgently and they couldn't favour this person as they knew others would have an issue or object to it.

When he approached me, I asked him why he did not apply earlier. He had no answer. I understood that it was negligence on his part. But at the same time, it was a genuine need, his need was not invented or made up nor was the urgency. Now, the only options that I had were, first, to ask him to apply and let the process take its due course and second, to expedite everything, calling people at block level, instructing staff and officers at my office and then following up on it to ensure that it is done on time, that is, he gets the certificate the same day. Now, the only acceptable part was that he has applied for it and that he has submitted the hard copy of the application as well and it was complete in all aspects. But, formalities still remained, once an application is made it has to go through several officers to reach me and then the certificate is issued. But surely there wasn't time for the regular pace of things.

I was getting all kinds of advice, from officers telling me not to entertain this special request and that it was not our fault that he was applying on the last day to staff not understanding the gravity of the matter or situation. I could see where they were coming from, it would be almost impossible for them if similar requests started to come daily and how would then they be able to say no to anyone and who would they say no to and who would they agree to help, on what parameters? But would that mean that we don't help the person in need, the person who has reached out and who needed this, it is not that he could go somewhere else if not us, only my office could issue the certificate. In this case, to me at least, there was no dilemma, once I saw the application and that it was complete in all aspects, I didn't see any reason as to why I should not issue the certificate.

I have always believed that anyone who is able to reach our offices with a legitimate request must be helped, simply because many of those who need us are still not able to access us, though technology has bridged the gap. However a huge population and remote locations still make for most people not being able to even reach the right office, and when they do, how many are actually able to see us is also a question. So, when someone does manage to reach out and has a legitimate issue, I don't see why they should not be helped. For this particular case, it wasn't actually much of a hassle, it must be noted it wasn't as it was just one such case, had it been hundreds of people asking for the same the same day, it would be impossible. But it was one case and it was not much of a problem apart from the fact that staff who have already refused him were now asked to help him and thus their egos were slightly bruised. But then it was not our job to take things personally and they had no choice but to help him.

Finally he was given the certificate after a few hours and following the due process and he thanked me personally, all I had to say to him was it would be better if he gave us at least a few days next time and we both smiled and parted amicably.

❖❖❖

CHAPTER 12

A Soldier Calls

"A soldier is away from home, serving the nation, fighting for a bigger idea, hoping that in his absence, his loved ones have the entire nation in their time of need".

Ask any IAS officer and almost every single one would agree on the "Bharat Darshan" being the most memorable part of their training. Bharat Darshan is a two month long India wide tour for IAS officers which they are taken on in their training as part of the effort to make them familiar with the rich culture and diversity of the nation, to understand and see the people they are going to serve and to learn how various departments and organisations function.

But Bharat Darshan has many components, all of them unique and wonderful in their own right, the most beautiful though is surely the attachment with the Indian army. Different groups of IAS trainees are taken to various states with international borders and they are exposed to the very real ground working of the army and the armed forces.

We were also taken to our army attachments and we had it in the beautiful state of Jammu and Kashmir, it was then a state. As surreal as the experience was, we were treated extremely kindly by the army and the senior officers who met us and spared time to speak to us on various aspects of national security and workings of the Indian Army, all of which was amazing. We were all in awe of the discipline, the professionalism, the sense of honour and duty among the ranks and we were very happy to interact with not just officers but soldiers as well, they were the real heroes for us.

I remember that each sub group of 4-5 officers was assigned a soldier to help them navigate through the early days of the attachment. It was here that I first met Mujibur.

He was a soldier in the Indian army, at the time posted at Srinagar where we had gathered initially in our attachment to be later sent to our outposts. He was not assigned to our group but to another one, we met him as one of my batchmates brought him over to where our group was and introduced him to me. The reason for this was that he was from West Bengal and I was going to the West Bengal cadre. I was the only one from the West Bengal cadre in our Bharat Darshan group so they thought of introducing him to me. He was very respectful and kind and I was the same to him, he was already serving the nation, so far away from his home, he deserved all our respect and love.

It was after many such meetings that we understood and were even told that the real purpose of our attachment with the armed forces was not just to understand the nuances of different dimensions of national security and the working and functioning of the Indian army but to understand and see for ourselves the sacrifices that our soldiers make for us daily and develop a more humane outlook towards them.

All of us would go on to serve in different districts, sub divisions, cities, towns, municipal corporations, across the country and we would find families with their sons and daughters in the army everywhere. Families who had sent away their loved ones and each day for them was a lifetime, a lifetime of waiting for them to come back. We were to understand their pain and empathise with them, which was of course the least that they deserved.

So, after talking to him, I gave him my card, asking him to text or call me whenever he needed any help. Our army attachment continued and it was easily one of the finest experiences of our lives and we all still cherish the memories.

After our training was complete and we were finally sent to the field, I was posted as SDM at Kandi, Murshidabad. A big rural sub division with a sizeable population, it was in fact as large as many districts in other states. One unique feature of the place was that it had many young men serving in the armed forces. Thus, visits and requests by the families of the soldiers were very frequent. Most of these concerned land disputes and other similar family matters.

That is when one day I got a message, the message was an image and a text, the image was of my old listing card and the text just read, "Jai Hind, sir! I am Mujibur". I knew who it was and replied asking him to give me a call. He gave me a call, I responded and the voice on the other end went, "Jai Hind, sir!", to which I replied, "Jai Hind, please tell me, Mujibur". The voice which was of a man went, "Sir, it has been 4 years, I don't know if you remember, I am Mujibur, I met you in Jammu and Kashmir when you came to visit during your training". I had already recognised him and said, "of course I remember you, how are you doing?". He answered, "Sir, I am fine, how are you". I said, "I am very well, thank you. Please tell me, how can I help you, is everything all right? He heard my words and I could sense the relief and happiness in his voice.

He said, "Sir, I wanted to tell you that you are posted at Kandi and my home is also at Kandi, my whole family lives in your jurisdiction and they only called me and told me about you". I smiled, and said, "Oh, that is such a pleasant surprise, I am happy to hear this, please feel free to call me if you need any help and also share this number with your family." He was ecstatic and said, "Sir, that is enough for us, I don't need any help but that you offered your number and showed me such respect and warmth, I'm am very happy". I was still wondering how and why would his family tell him about an SDO posted in his area, so I asked him, "Mujibur, do your family need any help, please say, why were they telling you about me"?

He was silent for a split second and replied, "Sir, there is no point in concealing it from you, actually my family is facing an issue and that is why they called me asking me to try and ask my commanding officer to write a letter to you to help my family, that is when they mentioned your name and I recognised you in a second. I told them I'd message you, all of them were so happy".

I knew he needed some help so I asked him again, "that's really great, Mujibur, now please tell me what help do your family need"?

He said, "Sir, my family is being harassed by our neighbours, they are not allowing my family to construct a room on our own land, we have all the relevant permits and papers, still they have been threatening and not allowing the work to start".

He told me about the whole issue and it didn't seem like a major problem, for me to sort out. For him of course it was an issue as he was not there and his family was being troubled. So I asked him to not worry and told him to text me the name and number of any person from his family and I would take care of the matter.

He was delighted and thanked me profusely, it was wonderful to talk to him but what I really remember is the fact how he wasn't willing to tell me why he actually called. It was polite and kind of him even though what he was asking me was not a favour but a part of my job but that humility was still remarkable.

I personally called the number he sent me and arranged for the issue to be taken care of, it was not a very complicated problem and did not take much time. He called me again to thank me and we are still I touch, he replies to my stories on whatsapp and apparently likes my paintings, I always reply back, I like to believe, just for a moment, once I do, he smiles.

❖❖❖

CHAPTER 13

Three Principles of Honesty

"An honest officer is not afraid, all reasons for an officer to be afraid stem from the desires of things that are not his".

One of the most common misconceptions about civil services around the globe and more so in India is the fact that it is impossible for anyone to remain honest, that the "system" is such that no one can remain honest, that either they are corrupt or the system makes them impossible to remain honest.

Nothing can be farther away from the truth. Honesty is not in the grey ever, I get these examples on how this officer though is honest but due to him not being "flexible" many things couldn't be done or accomplished or how much more he could have done if he had just compromised a little and had he been more flexible. The issue with this line of argument is, we are no one to be flexible in the face of law and rules, more so when the benefit from this flexibility would not lie with the vulnerable.

Being honest and having unshakable integrity would never come in anyone's way of being an exemplary officer, in fact these are the real prerequisites of being one.

As an Indian Administrative Service (IAS) officer, I can attest to the significance of honesty in the Civil Services in India. Honesty is a value that is ingrained in the ethos of the IAS, and it forms the bedrock of our service to the nation. The IAS is one of the most prestigious and sought-after civil services in India, and with that comes a tremendous responsibility to uphold the highest standards of ethics and integrity.

IAS officers are entrusted with the responsibility of implementing government policies and programmes effectively and efficiently. In doing so, we have to work with a range of stakeholders, including politicians, fellow bureaucrats, private sector, civil society and the public at large. The job is challenging and comes with a significant amount of power as well, which can easily be misused if we are prepared to compromise on our honesty and integrity.

Corruption is a pervasive issue in India, and it has been a significant obstacle to the country's progress, there can be no debate about whether corruption exists, it does and there is no running away from it. In fact most officers themselves would narrate at least one incident where they faced the prospect of bribing someone before they became officers.

As IAS officers, we are in a position to combat corruption and make a real difference in the lives of people. However, this can only be achieved if we hold ourselves to the highest standards of honesty and integrity. Corruption not only undermines public trust in the government but also has a detrimental effect on the economy and society at large.

Unfortunately, there have been instances where IAS officers have compromised their honesty at times what is labelled "for the sake of pragmatism and practicality". I would still maintain and say that these are not the majority, they are exceptions. Some officers may believe that they need to compromise their values to get things done in a bureaucratic system that is notorious for being slow and inefficient. However, this approach is short-sighted and can have severe consequences in the long run.

For instance, an IAS officer may be tempted to accept a bribe to expedite a project that is crucial for the public. While this may seem like a pragmatic solution to get things done quickly, it sets a dangerous precedent that undermines the rule of law and weakens the foundations of democracy. Accepting bribes erodes public trust in the government and creates a culture of impunity. Also, when there are rules more so when it comes to public finance, we are in no position to show this flexibility.

As IAS officers, we have to recognise that we are the custodians of public trust and have a duty to serve the public interest. We must hold ourselves to the highest standards of ethics and integrity, and we cannot compromise our values for the sake of pragmatism. We must act in a manner that is transparent, accountable, and free from any conflict of interest.

In fact, I don't buy or agree with this whole argument of "system corrupting you" and that the "non-corrupt can't survive", it is absolutely not true. Most officers are honest and just because the corrupt make the most amount of noise. They get undue attention and bring an unacceptable or shoddy name to the entire service.

Honesty is the most essential component for the Civil Services, and it cannot be compromised for the sake of pragmatism or practicality or to get things done or anything like that. As IAS officers, we have a responsibility to uphold the highest standards of integrity and ethics and work towards eradicating corruption from the system. The public expects and deserves honest, accountable, and transparent governance, and it is our duty to deliver it. We must remember that honesty is not just a virtue but a duty that we owe to the people of India.

Thus, being a firm believer in this, I had to devise my own way of filtering things and decision-making process, in order to never compromise with anything.

I call this system "the three principles of honesty" system. First, never indulge in anything yourself, that would mean that no matter what, you would not participate or entertain anything in the domain of dishonesty or compromise. Second, never ignore anything in this domain when brought to your notice, no matter by whom, you have to take action as per rules. And, third, your subordinates indulging in corruption are also your responsibility and you can't just wash your hands of it by saying you can't control or oversee everyone working under you.

What actually happens if one follows these three steps or rules is that not only is he or she saving himself and discharging his duties but at the same time, he or she is also creating a system which can last long after he leaves his office and goes on to work at another place. These three simple steps can ensure a cleaner system and the governance that the people deserve.

❖❖❖

CHAPTER 14

Art is for Your Heart

"For a world built on code, art is its soul".

Art has been a part of human society for thousands of years, it was in fact thc first medium of expression, language developed much later as a way to communicate and connect, it was just art what we had for many years. From the cave paintings of prehistoric times to the modern art movements of today, art has played a crucial and key role in our culture, society, and individual lives. However, in today's fast-paced and technology-driven world, art has taken a back seat, and people are often too busy with their daily routines to engage in artistic endeavours, they are too preoccupied to notice and appreciate the beauty of any art forms. It is just this nature of today's existence that makes it even more crucial for people to recognise the importance of art in today's world and the power it holds to fill our hearts with love and joy and make us more sensitive towards fellow humans and other creations of nature.

Art, in all its forms, is glorious, it is the highest form of human enterprise, it has the power to transform and inspire people. It can create a sense of wonder and awe, evoke emotions, and offer a new perspective on the world and everything around us and beyond. Art can be a means of self-expression, a way to communicate complex ideas and emotions, and a tool for cultural and social commentary. In today's world, where people are often disconnected from each other and the natural world, art can offer a way to reconnect and create a sense of belonging.

I have long appreciated this power and always wanted to pick up art and various art forms in true earnest. But, like most people, I was always "too busy" for it to happen. Yes, it was almost like something which will happen and not something which I will have to take active steps to make it happen.

I had studied arts in my school and I was not adept at it but I wasn't bad. It was one of those things which always fascinated me enough for me to make concerted efforts but the school education system's of making even art a rote learning process killed any enthusiasm that I had for it.

After I left school and joined IIT Roorkee, the campus itself being a work of art and add to that some of the most creative people in the country in the campus, you get an explosion of creativity. IIT Roorkee gave me an opportunity to explore the other side of my creativity where I was deep diving into graphic design, with my best friend, designing posters and t-shirts and greeting cards. It worked so well and successfully that we decided to have our own start-up. We launched it as well and ran it for one whole year before we closed for no other reason but inability to work together as a team. Then as college ended and I got into UPSC preparation the art took a back seat. I regret it to this day, it was not that I didn't have time but I just somehow painted it as an activity which I didn't "need to do".

After selecting though, I went to LBSNAA and yet again, the campus was a work of art and yet again some of the finest minds stayed in such close vicinity. Some of them were very creative and it didn't take long for the spark to reignite itself. I was spellbound by the natural beauty of LBSNAA but at the same time I was also in love with the creative air. There is something about the place which can make an artist out of anyone. I was happy to feel it again but the real experiment began once I joined my cadre and started working in the field.

I have always been fascinated by art, so much so that I have read three different biographies of Leonardo da Vinci. I love all forms and all art equally and find them all beautiful in their own ways.

Artistic endeavours can range from traditional art forms like painting, sculpture, and drawing to more contemporary forms like photography, film, and digital art. They also include performing arts like music, dance, and theatre. Whatever the medium, engaging in artistic endeavours can have significant benefits for individuals and I for one have long appreciated the power of art.

I am also lucky that my wife is also very creative and loves crafts and making things with her hands and appreciates all handmade items. We started doing things together, painting together, sketching together, gardening, making and painting pots, making crafts and a lot more. It was and still is like meditation to us.

One of the most significant benefits of engaging in art for us has been its ability to promote mental health and well-being. Studies have shown that art can reduce stress and anxiety, increase positive emotions, and even alleviate symptoms of depression and it is something that we have witnessed first hand as well. Art can offer a sense of purpose, fulfilment, and meaning to our lives as well. Engaging in artistic endeavours can also improve cognitive function and enhance problem-solving skills, creativity, and innovation, all of this is absolutely scientific and numerous studies exist which prove this. I always believed and continue to do so that embracing art is one of the surest ways to a healthier lifestyle.

This is the reason why I paint, sketch and design and try my hand at whatever new form I can and try my best to give it my own spin.

All of us are aware that art can also serve as a means of cultural and social commentary. It can provide a platform for the marginalized voices and offer a way to challenge social norms and values. Art can be used to raise awareness about social and political issues, promote social justice, and bring people together in solidarity. In today's world, where social and political issues are becoming increasingly polarized, art can offer a way to bridge the divide and promote understanding and empathy.

Art has the power to fill hearts with love and joy. I have seen it myself and experienced it as well, those few hours spent painting or sketching or creating things are spent with great happiness. Art can evoke emotions and offer a sense of beauty and wonder in the world. Whether it is a beautiful painting, a moving piece of music, or a powerful performance, art can offer a sense of transcendence and awe that can uplift the human spirit. In today's world, where people often feel disconnected and alienated, art can offer a way to connect with others and create a sense of community and belonging.

Art is more essential in today's world than it ever was in any other era, it is crucial for people to engage in artistic endeavours.

By engaging in artistic endeavours, we can enrich our lives and contribute to the betterment of society. We must recognise the importance of art in our lives and make an effort to incorporate it into our daily routines. Whether it is taking a painting class, attending a concert, or visiting a museum, we must make time for art in our lives and allow it to inspire, transform, and uplift us.

❖❖❖

CHAPTER 15

Writing is for Your Peace

"Taking a pen and spilling all your thoughts on paper is the surest way to find peace".

In today's world, with the rise of digital communication and technology, writing has become an undervalued art form. It is evident that people rely increasingly on digital devices and communication tools, neglecting the importance of writing things down. However, from my own personal experience and which is attested to by some much more famous and successful people, the habit of writing is not only crucial for our productivity and making us better at our job, it can bring significant emotional and creative benefits to individuals, more so in today's world.

As we know, writing can take many forms, from jotting down notes in a meeting to keeping a personal journal. It can also include writing letters, making lists, and even doodling, all of this is writing and all of it is good. The act of writing allows individuals to externalise their thoughts and ideas, making them tangible and easier to remember. When we have something in front of us and not just in our head any more, it has already gone one step ahead from being a random, hazy idea to something more concrete. Writing also allows individuals to reflect on their experiences and emotions, helping them to process and understand their feelings better and to know and judge why they felt what they did and why they acted in the way they did.

In my personal experience, one of the most significant benefits of writing things down has been its ability to provide a sense of peace and tranquillity. To me, writing is a meditative practice that allows me to focus my mind and find a sense of calm. It also helps me to let go of negative thoughts and emotions and cultivate a sense of gratitude and positivity.

Writing is an incredibly powerful tool for self-discovery and personal growth. By writing down their thoughts and feelings, individuals can gain a deeper understanding of themselves and their values, what they are, what they stand for, what actually matters to them and much more.

Writing allows individuals to explore their beliefs and ideas and refine their thinking. They get the benefit of hindsight when they revisit their notes or writings and understand themselves and their decision-making better. Writing can also help individuals to set goals and develop a plan to achieve them.

Moreover, writing for me, has been a means of therapy. Keeping a personal journal or notebook helps me to process my emotions and work through difficult experiences or negative situations much better. It gives me a way to vent out all negativity and reflect better. Writing allows me to express myself freely and without judgment, providing an outlet for emotions that may be difficult to express in other ways.

Writing can also help individuals to gain a new perspective on their experiences and find meaning in difficult situations.

In addition to promoting personal growth and healing, writing can also foster creativity and innovation. Writing allows individuals to generate new ideas and perspectives, opening up new possibilities for problem-solving and innovation. Writing can also help individuals to identify patterns and connections between seemingly unrelated ideas, leading to new insights and breakthroughs.

I for one have been running a blog for more than 12 years now. I made it when I was still early days into my college and it was just meant for myself back then. I used to and continue to make a note of my thoughts, learnings, experiences and everything else. It has been a constant companion and it is a treasure to me, a way to look at my personal journey and growth like no other.

Writing can also be a means of advocacy, more so in the world of digital lives, allowing individuals to express their opinions and raise awareness about important issues.

For me, writing is a crucial practice, more so in today's world. I always say and maintain that writing can help individuals to find peace and tranquillity, promote personal growth and healing, foster creativity and innovation, and allow for much better communication and advocacy.

Writing can also be a means of self-discovery and a tool for personal growth. By making writing a part of their daily routine, individuals can unlock their full potential and lead a more fulfilled life. I have tried to do the same and I won't say how good or bad I am in my opinion but I am certainly a better person because of this habit.

❖❖❖

CHAPTER 16

Weights are for Your Body

"A lot of stress is given to physical well-being, but only when we are no longer in the position to do much about it".

Fitness and me have a very strange connection. I was always, as far back as I can remember, an athlete. I used to enjoy almost all sports, football, cricket, badminton, volleyball, track and field events and I was also into taekwando, a form of martial arts. This continued well into college and I was almost always on the football field. Due to this, I was never an obese child, I was always super thin, athletic, but I was at the same time perhaps too thin, I remember I used to weigh 54 kgs in college in the first and second year.

It was in my third year that I started to think and worry about my weight and overall fitness. I was of course fit as far as being well in the conventional sense was concerned but I was grossly underweight and to be honest, the major reason for me to worry about it was my performance on the football field. Being too thin though had its advantages in say pace and movement, football is surely a game of strength as well. That is when I decided to gain weight and began working out seriously and regularly. Thus my journey with weight training began in college in the third year and it has since been almost a decade. The journey has been one full of learning, ups and downs and immense satisfaction. It has made me into a man who values physical fitness immensely and respects those who take extra and special care of this aspect.

As we can all see, in today's fast-paced world, where people have busy or to be precise chaotic schedules and sedentary lifestyles, physical fitness has become more critical than ever before. With the rise of desk jobs and technology, people often find themselves sitting for long hours and not engaging in enough physical activity, it is rightly said that "sitting is the new smoking". This practice can lead to various health-related issues, including but not limited to obesity, heart disease, and diabetes. In such a scenario, weight training and workout can play a crucial role in improving overall health, promoting a healthy body and mind, and enhancing the general level of well-being.

For context, weight training is a form of strength training that involves using weights or resistance to build muscle and improve strength. It is an essential component of fitness and has numerous benefits for the body and mind. Weight training can help individuals to burn fat, increase muscle mass, and improve overall body composition. It can also help to improve bone density, reduce the risk of injury, and improve joint mobility.

One of the most significant benefits of weight training is its ability to improve overall health. Weight training can help individuals to reduce the risk of chronic diseases, including heart disease, diabetes, and obesity. It can also help to lower blood pressure, reduce cholesterol levels, and improve cardiovascular health. For people in their late 20s and early 30, it is crucial to make this a part of their routine right now. Moreover, weight training can help to improve mental health by reducing stress and anxiety levels and improving overall mood. We know that mental health is much less talked about and is often not considered an illness. Though it should be noted that mental health issues often crop up in an unhealthy body and environment.

For sports freaks like me, weight training can also help to improve athletic performance, unlike many believe, it won't slow you down. By increasing strength and endurance, weight training can help individuals to perform better in sports and other physical activities. It can also help to improve balance, coordination, and agility, leading to better overall athletic performance.

Moreover, weight training can help to improve bone density and reduce the risk of osteoporosis. As people age, their bones become weaker and more susceptible to fractures. Weight training can help to improve bone density and reduce the risk of osteoporosis, leading to better overall bone health and a reduced risk of fractures. This helps you to stay biologically younger and fitter for much longer.

Apart from weight training, working out in general, with or without equipment is also a very effective way to improve overall health and well-being. Working out can involve a range of activities, including running, cycling, swimming, and other cardiovascular exercises. These activities can help to improve overall fitness, promote weight loss, and improve mental health.

Cardiovascular exercise can help to improve cardiovascular health, reduce blood pressure, and improve cholesterol levels. It can also help to reduce the risk of developing type 2 diabetes and some forms of cancer.

Moreover, working out can help to improve mental health by reducing stress and anxiety levels and improving overall mood. Exercise releases endorphins, which are natural mood-boosters, leading to a sense of well-being and increased energy levels. Working out can also help individuals to improve their sleep patterns, leading to better overall health and well-being.

Weight training and working out can help individuals to improve their overall quality of life. By promoting physical fitness, weight training and working out can lead to improved self-confidence, higher energy levels, and a greater sense of well-being. This, in turn, can lead to better more cordial relationships, greater career success, and a more fulfilling life.

Many aspirants and students who reach out to me, full time or working professionals, ask and often complain that they are not able to find time for workouts in their daily schedule which includes 10-12 hours of study/work, 7 hours of sleep and study as well other things. They ask how on earth did I manage to work out during preparation.

The reason why I was able to do it was the fact that I had included my gym and fitness routine in my daily regular timetable and have made the rest of the schedule around it. I did not intend to fit in work out time in my study time table, but I made mystery timetable around my work out time. It was and remains my priority, in the actual sense of the word.

After being posted in the field, I had regained a sense of my old self and have started making health an actual priority, so much so that everything comes second to me, it must, unhealthy me can't do anything well, it makes no sense to ignore it. I have again built my daily routine around my gym timings and all other activities have to be around it and adjust to it. I don't miss workout for parties/ celebrations/outings/shopping, etc ever. This time I am not letting it slip again.

❖❖❖

CHAPTER 17

Solitude is for Your Soul

"If you can't stay alone and be happy in your own company, no one else can make you happy".

In the IAS, specifically when you are an outsider, working away from your family, from your roots, from your friends, from you culture, you have no choice but to embrace being alone in a world where you are supposedly always in the limelight. Solitude for me has been a blessing, the time I have been alone to reflect and grow as a result has and continues to be precious.

Don't take me wrong here, I love my family, I never go a day without speaking to each member of my family, what I mean is, the alone time which I have got as a result of the remote postings and a cadre far away from home state and no leave to go home, I have used it well.

In the world that we live in today, people are constantly surrounded by noise, distractions, and most worryingly demands and expectations from others. The technology boom has though brought people together, it has, at the same time, taken away any time people used to have for themselves. The fast-paced lifestyle of modern times often leads people to forget the importance of solitude and spending time with oneself. When I mean time with oneself, I don't mean sitting alone in a group lost in one's phone scrolling mindlessly. Solitude is a vital component of our well-being and can have profound effects on our physical, mental, and spiritual health. Solitude is often misunderstood as loneliness, which is the feeling of being isolated from others. Solitude, on the other hand, is the experience of being alone without feeling lonely. It is the state of being comfortable with oneself and not seeking distractions or stimulation from external sources. The benefits of solitude are numerous and can have a significant impact on our lives.

Spending time with oneself can help us to develop a deeper understanding of our own emotions, thoughts, and values. In a world where we are constantly bombarded with information and distractions, it is easy to lose sight of what truly matters to us. Solitude allows us to reflect on our own lives, understand our own needs, and make better decisions. It can also help us develop greater empathy towards others by giving us a better understanding of our own emotions and how they affect us. For me, solitude has helped me understand what is truly important to me, it has also made me more calm as a person, it has given a comfortable silence about my existence.

Then, solitude can have profound effects on our mental health. In today's world, anxiety, stress, and depression are no longer things which are known but not spoken about, they are in fact on the rise. Many people find it challenging to switch off and relax, leading to burnout and a lack of productivity. Solitude can be an effective way of managing stress and anxiety, allowing us to recharge our batteries and take a break from the demands of our ultra-modern life. It can also help us develop resilience and coping strategies for dealing with difficult and complex situations.

Also, spending time with oneself can lead to us having spiritual experiences and see actual growth. Many spiritual traditions emphasize the importance of solitude and meditation as a way of connecting with a higher power. Now you don't need to be a believer to experience this, a higher power in this case can be your own inner self. Solitude can help us develop a deeper sense of meaning and purpose in our lives, allowing us to connect with something greater than ourselves. It can also help us develop greater awareness and mindfulness, leading to a more fulfilling and meaningful life.

Solitude can have a positive impact on our physical health as well. Research has shown that spending time in nature, which often involves being alone, can lower blood pressure, reduce inflammation, and boost the immune system. Solitude can also be a way of engaging in physical activities that promote well-being, such as yoga, meditation, or exercise. By focusing on our own physical health, we can also improve our mental and emotional health, leading to a better overall sense of well-being. I would also suggest painting or sketching or writing or reading alone in nature, the power of these activities is just immense and beneficial.

Finally, solitude can help us develop stronger relationships with others. By taking the time to understand ourselves, we can better understand others and their needs. Solitude can also help us develop greater empathy, compassion, and understanding towards others, leading to stronger and more meaningful relationships.

However, despite the many benefits of solitude, many people find it challenging to spend time alone. The modern world is designed to keep us constantly connected and stimulated, making it difficult to disconnect and switch off. Additionally, many people may feel guilty or ashamed of wanting to spend time alone, feeling that it is a sign of weakness or anti-social behaviour or depression or they might just be having what is known as FOMO or Fear Of Missing Out.

To overcome these barriers, it is essential to cultivate the habit of spending time alone regularly. This can be done in many ways, such as going for a walk, practising yoga, meditating, or simply sitting quietly and reflecting. It is also essential to let go of any guilt or shame associated with spending time alone, recognizing that it is a vital part of our well-being. Trust me, giving yourself a break from your phone, computer and TV and spending that time with your own self would make you a happier and healthier person in a matter of days.

❖❖❖

CHAPTER 18

Always a Student

"The moment you stop learning, you stop living, you exist but you stop living".

People often ask me, why am I so restless and why am I always trying my hand at new things and trying to make sense of as many things as possible. I am not just restless though, I am always super excited, boredom is not something which I have felt for a long time. The main reason behind this is the fact that I see the Universe in a different light, I don't see it as something where I am stuck or I have to do something but as a playground, where the rides are just endless. I always try to keep the inquisitive and curious child in me alive, I have always been the question asking kind and I have always been happy this way, seeking answers makes me happy.

But it is most important thing that perhaps makes me do this with ease is the fact that I don't do this to please anyone or make an impression or any external validation, I do it because it genuinely makes me happy. I do it because it gives me a sense of wonder and fills my heart with awe and amazement as I look at this wonderful world around us and the opportunities to learn and grow that we have.

But it is not the same for most people. In these times where technology is advancing at such a rapid pace and industries are changing constantly, it has become essential for everyone to engage in constant experimenting and rediscovering, not just for the sake of a job or security but also to avert an existential crisis. By constantly learning and exploring new things, people can be more creative, stay ahead of the curve, and succeed in their endeavours.

First and foremost, constant experimenting and rediscovering is essential for any who wishes to stay ahead in today's ever-changing world and wishes to have a sense of security. This is speaking from a strictly professional point of view but it is not limited to that, even to stay ahead or upto the mark in your personal life, in the complicated times that we live in, with technology taking over all aspects of our lives. This experimenting and trying new things can very well have a positive impact on you having better relationships.

Speaking strictly in terms of future of work, with technology advancing so rapidly, industries are changing faster than ever before. For example, with the advent of automation and artificial intelligence, many jobs that were once considered secure are now being replaced by machines. As a result, it has become crucial for people to constantly learn new skills and explore new opportunities to stay ahead of the curve.

Moreover, experimenting and rediscovering can also make people more creative. When people engage in constant learning and exploration, they are exposed to new ideas and perspectives that can spark their creativity. For example, an artist who constantly experiments with different mediums and techniques is more likely to create something truly unique and innovative, doesn't mean someone who sticks with just one thing won't be able to attain the same level of efficiency but genius is often more of a tinkerer.

In addition to staying ahead and being creative, constant experimenting and rediscovering can also lead to greater levels of overall satisfaction and happiness. When people are constantly learning and exploring, they are more likely to find activities and pursuits that they truly enjoy. For example, someone who tries out different hobbies and activities may discover a love and appreciation for hiking or painting, which can provide them with a sense of purpose and fulfilment. I am sure all of us have heard many people tell them that they don't know what their calling is or what they are meant to do or what their purpose is. The reason for this is them being stuck in conventions and not trying new things and just being comfortable and not taking any risk. Constantly experimenting and rediscovering can also lead to a more fulfilling career. By exploring new skills and opportunities, people can find careers that align with their passions and values, rather than simply settling for a job that pays well or worse one which was chosen for them by their parents or peers. This can lead to greater levels of job satisfaction and overall life satisfaction.

However, it is important to note that constant experimenting and rediscovering can be a challenging process and it is not easy for most people. It requires people to be open-minded, adaptable, and willing to take risks. Many people may feel comfortable sticking to what they know and avoid exploring new opportunities, but this can lead to stagnation and missed opportunities. Times change and times are changing very fast it is something which every generation hears but this time the change is at an unprecedented rate.

I am an IAS officer, a service which most people choose for the security it offers as a career, this in has both effects, it is a paradox. On the one hand the security makes the officers work impartially and fearlessly and work only what laws required them to but on the other hand it does to an extent make officers easily satisfied though most officers go on to get further degrees and finish numerous courses, it is an issue nonetheless overall. I for one have made a point to constantly upgrade my skills and remain up to date.

It is essential for people to embrace a growth mindset and a willingness to learn and explore. They can do this by setting aside time for regular learning and exploration, such as taking classes or attending workshops or taking online courses, or forming peer groups. Additionally, they can seek out mentors or peers who can provide guidance and support.

Constant experimenting and rediscovering is essential in today's world. It allows people to stay ahead of the curve, be more creative, find greater levels of satisfaction and happiness, and pursue more fulfilling careers. While it can be a challenging process, it is well worth the effort. By embracing a growth mindset and a willingness to learn and explore, people can unlock their full potential and lead more fulfilling lives.

❖❖❖

CHAPTER 19

Reading Like There's No Tomorrow

"Books, unlike people, always give, even when they expect things from you, it is only to give you a lot more".

Reading for me has become more than a mere hobby long back, it is an essential part of my existence. It is not just one of the activities which I undertake daily but I do it as a form of a higher calling. I have always believed in the power of knowledge and wisdom, knowledge of course can come from books but wisdom comes with lived experience, either or those in their own sense and standing are incomplete and need each other for a meaningful life.

Reading books is not just a way to know more on a topic for example, it is a way to explore new worlds, new ideas and new perspectives and dimensions. It is a way to expand our horizons and gain a deeper understanding of the world around us. Reading has the power to transport us to different times and places, to make us laugh or cry, to inspire us and to challenge us. It is a never-ending journey of discovery and growth.

As far back as I can see, I see myself reading a book. I have always been very grateful to my parents for everything that they have done for me but encouraging me to read the newspaper and books in general, and not just course books, any book, was perhaps the biggest contribution they had in making my mind what it is, that is curious and always exploring new things. I have been reading for decades now and each time I pick up a book, the feelings are the same, that of excitement, wonder and anticipation of what new things I will learn.

The joy of reading is something that cannot be described fully in words. It is an experience that has to be felt and lived. Reading has taught me so much about life, about myself and about others. It has helped me become a better person and has given me a deeper appreciation for the world we live in. It has made me a more open minded person, someone who is able to appreciate different perspectives and form an opinion after giving all of them their due.

Reading is not something which needs any efforts, not just for me, for anyone who does it with proper attention on the work and cuts out distractions and noises, reading is an activity which can make anyone leap from one world to another, leaving the real one for some time.

I also believe that reading is not only important and essential for personal growth but it is also crucial for our society as a whole, it is not something to be done by an individual for individual improvement but, it makes us better as a group of people. Reading can help us understand different cultures and lifestyles, and can broaden our horizons. It can also promote empathy and compassion towards others, as it allows us to see the world from different perspectives.

In today's digital age, where everything is consumed in bite-sized pieces and attention spans are decreasing, reading has become even more important. It allows us to slow down, to focus and to engage in deep thinking. It is an antidote to the fast-paced, instant gratification culture that surrounds us.

I have always been and will remain a dedicated advocate of reading as the best way to spend one's time. It is not just a time for one to add to their know-how about things but to reflect and introspect. Reading as an activity is not about learning new things or learning about things, it is about learning one's own self. Reading books is like a mirror which lets you see inside of yourself and see what you truly are.

It helps you understand your own mind and heart, and to develop your critical thinking and analytical skills.

Reading can also be a tremendous source of inspiration and motivation. It can help you see the world in a more positive light, and give you a sense of purpose and direction. I encourage everyone, young and old, to read as much as they can. Whether it's fiction or non-fiction, sci-fi or romance, reading has something to offer everyone. In fact, I for one never read just one book at a time, I read multiple books and I read books of different genres and different subject matter at the same time. It is wonderful to see how they compliment each other.

Reading is a way to explore new worlds, new ideas, and new perspectives. It is a never-ending journey of discovery and growth. Reading has taught me so much about life, about myself, and about others. It has helped me become a better person and has given me a deeper appreciation for the world we live in. Reading is not only important for personal growth but it is also crucial for our society as a whole. It can help us understand different cultures and lifestyles, broaden our horizons, and promote empathy and compassion towards others. In today's digital age, reading has become even more important as an antidote to the fast-paced culture that surrounds us.

Let me give you an example, when the movie *Dune* came out last year, I had already read the book long back. I was able to appreciate the movie on a much better scale and in a much better way, understanding the limitations of the medium of a movie and also the places where it did justice, I was able to connect better with both forms much better. The same happened with the Harry Potter books when I was a child, reading the books made the experience so much better.

Reading books is the best possible way to expand our horizons and gain a deeper understanding of the world around us. As far back as I can see, I see myself reading a book. The joy of reading as a child was an experience made me live and feel every second much better. I remember reading *War and Peace* as a kid and and just loving the work. I am not sure if I understood its true depth but it was an experience which I still cherish.

This feeling has remained with me and it is one of the most special feelings.

Now, in the end, how I manage to read so much is by always using breaks, travel time, the first thing in the morning for me is not scrolling my social media but reading for 30 minutes. I avoid TV series and movies as much as possible, not into trends and don't have to watch every new movie or series which comes out. This gives me a lot of time to read. I also keep multiple books handy, hard copies, kindle, on phone so that I never run out of options.

Another crucial reason and perhaps the most important one in my reading journey is the fact that I read for my own sake, to know more, learn and grow and not to get something tangible out of it, maybe that takes off the pressure and compulsion out of it and makes it play rather than work.

❖❖❖

CHAPTER 20

There is No Shortage of Time But Messed Up Priorities

"Time is not one of the most important things, it is the only important thing".

Have you ever wondered how after a while, people from the same group, who were under similar circumstances for most of their early lives, had the same education, went to the same schools and yet end up having vastly different lives? They end up having not just divergent careers but also very different personal lives. Now, of course these things are just too complicated and have too many variables for us to discuss. But one thing which remains common in both the sets of stories, the ones with a happy ending and the ones with a tragic one show these two sets of people used their time when they still had it.

When it comes down to it, time is the most valuable resource we have. Yet, it's also the most limited. We all have the same amount of hours in a day, but how we choose to use those hours can make a big difference in our lives. Successful people prioritize their time. They focus on what's important, and they don't waste time on things that don't matter. They make a plan and stick to it. On the other hand, those who end up with regrets tend to prioritize things that aren't important. They get caught up in distractions and fail to make the most of their time.

When we live in the times where customer is not only the king but also to an extent the slave at the same time when he has been given so many choices that it is perhaps no longer feasible to say that greater the number of choices the better it is for the consumer. It is not something I am just saying either, it is something which has been long debated by economists and to a great extent shown by behaviouralists to be true, that you give someone too many choices and they would do worse. The same is happening to us, we have so many things on our plate that we are not able to prioritise them, we confuse the important and what appears important. When everything is sold has "the only thing you need to do for sure shot results" or "the only programme you need to make you super productive" or "the documentary which will change your lives", we surely no longer know what is in fact important and what isn't.

How then do we get out of this hellhole? This bottomless pit of nonsense content thrown at us at the speed of light and yes it doesn't make time go slower but faster. My circle is incredibly small but I do know people who wish to learn so many things and want to try their hands on many new ideas but the trap is so hard to avoid, the trap of streaming services and scrolling senselessly on social media is just too much for most people to avoid and once you are trapped, its almost impossible to come out, but one can do that.

That is where time management comes in. Time management is crucial and perhaps more important now than ever. With so many distractions and choices, it is easy to lose focus on what's truly important. One of the simplest ways to prioritise our time is by making a to-do list and ranking tasks in order of importance. I do this daily, mostly at night for the following day or early morning. I re-evaluate the list at the end of the day and see how many of the top 5 tasks I was able to do. This activity can help you focus on what is necessary and reduce wasted time.

Another tip is to break big tasks into smaller ones to make them less daunting. I make multiple lists, I am a fan of lists and I make them very meticulously, the time I spend on making them saves me a lot more later on. I make one lists with Marco weekly targets, one with road daily targets and then one which is a detailed version of the second list, tasks broken down in sub-tasks.

This is just to give an idea on how I manage my time, it has become a habit for me now to keep track of my time and how I spend it. It does not mean that I have no fun or enjoyment. I do and it does not mean that I am not instinctive, I am but what it means is I don't get carried away or overdo anything which I might come to regret later.

What I have also been able to develop as a habit is the self-induced trigger to keep a track of my targets and see if I have already lost a lot of time without doing anything for the day, that would mean it is time to do something from the list.

The reason I am saying all this is because I see just too many people say that they don't have enough time in a day to both work, work out, give time to family, give time to self, pursue a hobby, read and do it all while having fun. The issue is that it's not the lack of time, it's the messed up priorities and a very bad and careless management of time.

❖❖❖